MARVEL STUDIOS

CAPTAIN AMERICA

THE FIRST AVENGER

Adapted by
Elizabeth Rudnick

Based on the Motion Picture Screenplay by
Christopher Markus & Stephen McFeely

Published by Marvel Press, an imprint of Disney Book Group. No part of this book may be reproduced or transmitted in any form or by any means, electronic or mechanical, including photocopying, recording, or by any information storage and retrieval system, without written permission from the publisher. For information address Marvel Press, 114 Fifth Avenue, New York, New York 10011-5690.

Printed in the United States of America

First Edition

1 3 5 7 9 10 8 6 4 2

V381-8386-5-11121

ISBN 978-1-4231-4307-9

MARVEL
NEW YORK

Certified Chain of Custody
35% Certified Forests,
65% Certified Fiber Sourcing
www.sfiprogram.org

SUSTAINABLE FORESTRY INITIATIVE

TONSBERG, NORWAY, 1942

It was a quiet night. The cobblestoned streets of the small Norwegian town were damp, lit by the occasional, dim light from a few lonely street lamps. Suddenly, the silence was broken by the sound of pounding footsteps. Two men raced onto the main street, their faces frozen with fear.

"Go and tell the keeper!" a man shouted to his friend Jan. "Hurry!"

As Jan raced toward a large tower at the other end of town, a huge tank rolled onto the street. Several soldiers jumped out of the tank. A logo portraying a skull with multiple tentacles was displayed on the side of the soldiers' uniforms. HYDRA had arrived.

Jan threw open the door to Castle Rock Tower. Inside, an older man stood waiting. He was the tower keeper. And he knew what Jan's arrival meant.

"They've come for it!" Jan said, gulping in air.

"Let them come," the tower keeper said. "They'll never find it."

As he spoke, they both heard the ominous clanking of tank wheels. They watched in horror as an armored war machine crashed through the wall, sending bricks and timber raining down. Soldiers wearing black uniforms, their faces hidden, stormed inside. A few steps behind them was a man with pale, waxy skin and sunken eyes. This was Johann Schmidt, one of HYDRA's most evil officers.

His eyes scanned the room and landed on a stone tomb lying in an ornate crypt. "It has taken me a long time to find this place," Schmidt said, turning to the tower keeper. "You should be commended."

Schmidt moved closer to the old man. The object he had been searching for was almost within his grasp. The Tesseract of Odin. An item that contained the power of gods. An item that would make him . . . immortal.

With determination, Schmidt strode over to the coffin. He easily lifted its stone lid and threw it to the ground. Inside, a skeleton held a crystal cube.

"The Tesseract was the jewel of Odin's treasure room," Schmidt said, picking up the cube and turning it over in his hand. "It is not a thing one buries."

In one swift move, Schmidt grabbed the tower keeper and raised him high above his head. Schmidt watched the man's eyes dart to the wall. There must be something there, Schmidt realized. Throwing the man aside, Schmidt walked over to it. A tree was carved into one of the wall's stones. But this wasn't just any tree. This was Yggdrasil, the Tree of the World. There was a serpent etched into the tree's roots. Reaching out, Schmidt pushed the creature's eyes. The stone moved aside to reveal a small wooden box. Slowly, Schmidt opened the box. Suddenly, a bright blue light filled the room, and the tower keeper groaned.

Schmidt had found the Tesseract. It had begun. . . .

MANHATTAN, NEW YORK · 1942

Far from Norway's cobblestoned streets, Steve Rogers stood in a small room in New York City, waiting. Again. This was the fifth time he had gone to a recruitment office to try and enlist in the army. The United States was at war, and he wanted to help. The only problem was, Steve wasn't exactly soldier material. He was small and frail, with poor eyesight and asthma. No one wanted him to be fighting.

But Steve wasn't about to give up.

Steve stepped forward and the doctor led him to another room. There, he began to scan Steve's file. Dozens of ailments had been checked off, and there were red *x*'s all over the file.

"Sorry, son," the doctor said. Then he stamped the file with a big 4F, which meant that, again, Steve was unqualified to enlist in the army.

A little while later, Steve sat in a dark movie theater. On the screen, images from the war flashed by in a newsreel.

Suddenly, from a few rows behind him, a man called out, "Jeez, play the cartoon already!"

Steve felt his heart begin to pound. What was this guy's problem? Then the guy added, "Let 'em clean up their own mess!"

That was it! Steve wasn't going to just sit around and let some guy insult soldiers. He stood up, turned, and said, "You want to shut up, pal?" Then Steve gulped.

His new "pal" was huge. And he looked really, really, mean.

What have I gotten myself into? Steve thought.

WHACK! Outside, in an alley behind the theater, Steve and the big man traded punches. Steve was small, but he managed to get in a few good hits. But the other guy was just too big for him. Steve grabbed the closest thing he could find—a garbage-can lid—and held it in front of him like a shield. The bully reached his arm back, ready to strike, when suddenly a hand grabbed hold of him, stopping his arm.

"What's with all the fighting?" a voice said. "Don't you know there is a war going on?"

Steve opened his eyes—he had clenched them shut in anticipation of the punch—and smiled. His best friend, James "Bucky" Barnes, stood there, dressed in his army uniform. In one smooth move, he kicked the big guy out of the alley and then went to help up Steve.

Bucky was scheduled to fly to England the next day with his unit—the 107th—and while he wouldn't admit it, he was nervous. If he had only one night left, Bucky wanted to do something fun.

Later that night, Bucky and Steve found themselves at the World Exhibition of Tomorrow. It contained inventions of millionaire industrialist Howard Stark. There were booths set up displaying futuristic-looking buildings, and a monorail glided almost soundlessly above them. There was an air of celebration, as though people hoped to find something good in the future despite the sad wartime present.

As they wandered, Steve tried to enjoy the night. But he was still thinking about that big, red 4F stamp. Glancing around, his eyes stopped on the Army Recruitment Pavilion. As if pulled by an invisible string, Steve made his way over.

"You're really going to do this now?" Bucky asked when he saw where his friend was heading. "It's my last night."

Steve shook his head. He knew Bucky would be fine. He'd find some pretty girls to talk to and have a better night without Steve. The two friends shook hands. This was good-bye for now, unless Steve's luck turned.

He headed into the pavilion.

IT IS ILLEGAL TO FALSIFY
YOUR ENLISTMENT FORM.

Entering the booth, Steve looked around. It wasn't like the other recruitment centers he'd been in. It was practically empty—except for an old man.

Seeing Steve, the man walked over. "So, you want to be a fighter, heh?" he asked in a German accent.

Steve raised an eyebrow. "You're with the army?" he asked, sounding doubtful.

"Doctor Abraham Erskine," the man said, nodding. "Special Scientific Reserve, US Army."

The doctor went and found Steve's file. He opened it, as five other doctors had in five other cities. "So you would fight, yes," Dr. Erskine observed. "But you are weak, you are very small."

Steve bit his tongue. Then Dr. Erskine laid out the file and picked up a stamp. Steve's heart began to race as the doctor said, "I can offer you a chance—only a chance."

Raising his hand, he pressed the stamp down on the paper. 1A!

Steve didn't really know what the SSR was, but he didn't care. He was in the army!

Steve and eleven other recruits were sent to Camp Lehigh. Next to the big, healthy recruits, Steve looked even smaller than usual. But he was determined to make it through training.

After the recruits met Agent Peggy Carter and Colonel Chester Phillips, the two people in charge of this division of SSR, they were sent right into training. Steve found himself navigating a tricky obstacle course. As he struggled over a wall and under barbed wire, Colonel Phillips shouted to the recruits. "Our goal is to create the finest army in history," he said. "But every army starts with one man. By the end of this week, we're going to choose that man."

Steve didn't know what that meant, but he wanted to be that man. He kept on running. The training continued.

One by one, the other recruits were were given the news that they would be dismissed. Soon, Steve was the only one left. He sat on his bunk in the now-empty barracks, excited—and a little worried. He wasn't sure how he'd been chosen.

"Why me?" Steve asked when Dr. Erskine joined him.

The older man sighed. He had not always been in the SSR, he told Steve. Not that long ago, he'd been a scientist working in Europe. While doing an experiment, he discovered a powerful serum that turned ordinary men into superhumans. Certain scientists had wanted to use this to create an indestructible army. One man in particular, Johann Schmidt, became obsessed with the serum. In a fit of rage, Schmidt injected it into himself—with disastrous results.

"The serum amplifies what is inside," Dr. Erskine said, finishing his story. "Good becomes great . . . bad becomes worse."

The whole time, Steve had listened, disbelieving. But Erskine was serious.

"This is why you were chosen," he said. "Whatever happens tomorrow, promise me you'll stay who you are. Not a perfect soldier . . . but a good man."

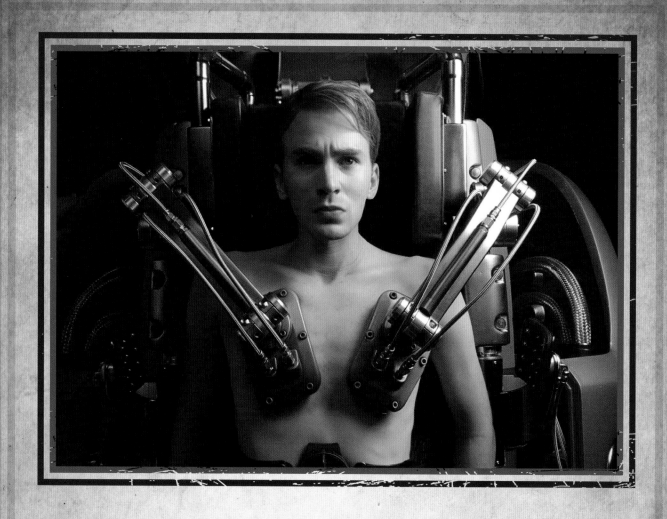

The next day, Steve found himself driving through Brooklyn, New York, with Peggy Carter. They pulled up in front of an antique store. This was the secret SSR headquarters for PROJECT: REBIRTH—the name given to the experiment that might just transform Steve into a Super-Soldier.

They walked through the store and down a flight of stairs. The lab stretched on and on, full of ultramodern equipment. Technicians operated machinery, while engineers manned monitors. A film crew set up in one corner of the room. Everyone looked up when Steve walked in. A lot was riding on him.

In the middle of the room there was a man-shaped cradle. This was the Rebirth device. Taking a deep breath, Steve walked over and got inside.

"Comfortable?" Dr. Erskine asked.

Steve nodded, and Erskine's attendants began hooking Steve up to various tubes. Above him, a group of men looked down from an observation booth. This was Senator Brandt and his aides. Brandt had helped get funding for the project and expected to see great results.

Steve gulped as a panel slid back to reveal seven vials of blue liquid. "Beginning serum infusion in five, four, three, two . . . one!" Dr. Erskine pressed a switch, and as everyone watched, Steve began to shake. Then his eyes started glowing blue.

When the vials were empty, the device's doors shut, sealing Steve inside the chamber. A piercing whine filled the air. Through a small window in the chamber, the others watched as Steve's face tensed. Then his eyes squeezed tight. Suddenly an orange glow filled the device, and Steve screamed.

"Kill the reactors!" Dr. Erskine cried.

But then, over the microphone, came Steve's voice, weak but audible. "No," he said. "I can do this."

Dr. Erskine swallowed nervously, but he pulled the lever down further. The orange light flashed a brilliant white, and then everything went dark.

The lab fell silent. Everyone held their breath as the chamber opened, waiting to see if the experiment had worked.

There was a gasp. Steve Rogers was no longer the skinny, frail man of before. Now he was muscular, tall, and physically perfect.

As the others rushed in and began congratulating one another, one of the men who had been up in the observation booth entered the lab. His gaze fell on the last remaining vial of serum. The man's eyes lit up. He pulled out a lighter and flipped it open, revealing a button.

Hearing the click, Dr. Erskine turned. His face grew pale. He knew this man. His name was Kruger, and he belonged to HYDRA. "NO!" Dr. Erskine shouted. But it was too late. The man hit a button and—BOOM!—the room exploded!

In the confusion, Kruger went for the serum. When Dr. Erskine tried to stop him, Kruger pulled out a gun and fired, hitting the scientist.

Steve, who was still recovering, watched his friend go down. "No!" he cried. Then, before Steve could stop him, Kruger grabbed the tube and raced out of the lab. Steve and Agent Peggy Carter leaped into action!

Outside, Kruger fired at Steve and Agent Carter, causing an explosion. Then he stole a cab and started to drive away. But Steve was fast now—superfast. In moments, Steve had caught up and jumped onto the car. As horns blared, Kruger sped through the streets, Steve clinging to the hood.

All of a sudden, a truck pulled out in front of them. Kruger jerked the steering wheel, hoping to miss the truck. The action caused the cab to flip and roll, taking Steve along with it.

When the cab came to a stop, Steve struggled to his feet while Kruger pulled himself out of the wreckage. Aiming his gun, the HYDRA agent fired. But Steve grabbed the cab's broken door and held it up in front of him like a shield.

Kruger turned and ran, making his way through a crowd of bystanders that had gathered and begun snapping pictures. He ducked and weaved, Steve right on his tail, until he made it to the end of a long pier.

After pulling out his lighter again, Kruger hit a button and a one-man submarine surfaced. Wasting no time, he got inside.

But Steve wasn't going to let him get away. He dove into the water and used all of his newfound strength to smash the cockpit's glass and pull Kruger out of the one-man submarine and up onto the pier. When they were on dry land, Steve threw Kruger to the ground. The vial of serum fell from Kruger's grasp.

"Who are you?" Steve asked, angry.

"The first of many," Kruger answered cryptically. "Cut off one head, and two more shall take its place. Hail HYDRA!" Then, as Steve watched, the man bit down on a cyanide pill, killing himself.

With a groan, Steve stood up. This day had turned out terribly. Even his new body and new strength couldn't make him feel better. He'd let down Erskine—and everyone else.

The next day, Steve found himself back in what was left of the SSR lab. Colonel Phillips paced furiously while Senator Brandt stood in the center of the room, unbothered by yesterday's events.

"I asked for an army!" Phillips raged, turning his attention on Steve. "All I got is you. It's not enough!"

But Brandt felt differently. He held up the day's newspaper. A picture of Steve battling Kruger was on the front page with a headline that read: MYSTERY MAN SAVES CIVILIANS. Steve's chase yesterday had gotten him attention. And that was what they needed. "You don't take a soldier—a symbol—like this and hide him in a lab," Brandt said.

Turning to Steve, he smiled. "Son, do you want to serve your country," he asked, "on the most important battlefield in this war?"

"It's all I want," Steve said, nodding.

Brandt's grin grew wider. "Then congratulations. You just got promoted."

The "promotion" wasn't exactly what Steve had in mind. A few days later, he found himself backstage in a small theater. He was wearing red boots and gloves, a blue costume covered with stars and stripes, and a mask with wings. He was an act, not a soldier.

The curtains parted and a group of dancing girls took to the stage singing, "He's the star-spangled man with the star-spangled plan, he's Captain America!" Then Steve nervously stepped out in front of the audience. There was practically no one there!

The show didn't stop, though. Brandt wanted to get people supporting the war, and Steve was his man. So Steve was sent to Buffalo and Milwaukee. He took the stage in San Francisco and St. Louis. At each city, the stories grew bigger, and so did the crowds. People were starting to talk about Captain America. He was a hero!

By the time his tour made it to New York City, Steve was no longer playing to small crowds. He sold out Radio City Music Hall. He was a bona fide hit!

And then Steve was sent to Italy, to the front lines of the war.

The show started the same way it always did—girls dancing, a bugle playing, and Captain America bursting onto the stage. But this time, when he came out and said, "I'm going to need a volunteer," he wasn't met with cheers. He was met with dead silence.

"I already volunteered," one of the soldiers finally shouted back. "How do you think I got here?"

Other soldiers started booing—and then one of them threw a tomato at Captain America. Ashamed, Steve fled the stage.

A little while later he sat on the now-empty bleachers, his head in his hands. What had he been thinking? He wasn't a hero. He was a joke.

Hearing the sound of footsteps, he looked up and saw Peggy Carter walking toward him. She took a seat next to him.

"You know," Steve said, "all I dreamed about was coming overseas, being with the men on the lines. And I finally get everything I wanted . . . and I'm wearing tights." He let out a deep sigh.

Peggy knew this was tough on Steve. She had grown fond of him over the past few months and wanted to make him feel better. But she had more bad news.

Johann Schmidt was moving through Europe, testing a new weapon. The US Army had sent in forces, but they had never returned. Then she told him the worst part. The missing company was the 107th—Bucky's division!

Steve raced off to Colonel Phillips's tent and burst inside. "I want to see the casualty list," he demanded.

Colonel Phillips didn't like Steve. And he didn't like getting

"orders" from him. But he felt he owed Steve the truth. "I'm sorry," he said.

A wave of anger washed over Steve. "What about the others?" he asked. "You're planning a mission, right?"

Phillips shook his head. They had to focus their attention on battles they could win. He dismissed Steve.

Outside Phillips's tent, Steve stood, shaking. He couldn't sit around and do nothing. He had joined the army to help people. And now he was going to do just that.

Later that night, Steve found himself in a big silver plane. Peggy sat across from him, debriefing him on what he had to do. The plane would drop him off almost right on top of a HYDRA factory where the prisoners were being kept.

Steve was nervous. His only training had been at Camp Lehigh, and he most certainly had never jumped out of a plane before. Or released a parachute. Or landed. He gulped.

"We're getting close to the drop zone!" a man called from the pilot's seat. Steve recognized the voice. He'd heard it on the radio. Just then, the pilot turned around and smiled. Steve had been right—it was playboy inventor and millionaire Howard Stark.

"Stark's the best civilian pilot I've ever seen," Peggy explained. "And just mad enough to brave this enemy airspace."

The plane shuddered under a barrage of bullets. They were being attacked! It was time for Steve to go. Strapping on his parachute, Steve made it to the door.

"Once I'm clear," Steve said, turning to Peggy, "turn this thing around and get out of here!"

Peggy shook her head. "You can't give me orders!" she shouted.

"Yes, I can," Steve said, flashing her his most charming smile. "I'm a captain!"

Then he jumped.

The wind whistled as Steve fell through the sky. Below him, the forest appeared to rush up, its tall trees looking like huge spears, ready to stab Steve. He had to slow down, or he'd be

in serious trouble. Pulling his parachute, he drifted down . . .
down . . . down . . . and suddenly—BOOM! Gunfire lit up the
night sky and tore a big hole in the chute.

Steve had no choice. Unhooking himself, he fell through the
trees to the ground. After he caught his breath, he stood up, his
legs shaky.

Though it hadn't been pretty, he had made it. But that
was the easy part. Now he had to get inside and rescue the
prisoners—and his best friend.

A few minutes later, Steve found himself outside the factory gates. Huge watchtowers were equipped with searchlights that scanned the ground and kept out any intruders. Steve could see HYDRA soldiers patrolling inside the perimeter.

Just then, three trucks drove up to the gate. Quietly, Steve ducked into the back of one. Then the truck rolled into the compound with Steve inside. When it came to a stop, Steve jumped out and stepped into the shadows. He waited.

Moments later, he spotted a group of prisoners being led across the compound toward a barrack. The men were beaten and bruised, but they were alive. Steve followed them inside the building. His jaw dropped. There were dozens of circular cages filling the space. And each one was filled with prisoners!

Creeping up behind one of the guards, Steve knocked him out with one Super-Soldier punch. Then he grabbed the keys and made his way down the cages, opening them one by one.

"Are there any others?" he asked when he was finished.

"The isolation ward," one of the soldiers answered.

Steve nodded. That was on the factory floor. He wasn't done yet.

The factory floor was full of guns, bombs, and half-packed crates. Inside some of the bombs, Steve saw cartridges that glowed blue, just like Dr. Erskine's serum. He pocketed a few before moving on. Outside, the first alarms sounded. Steve had to hurry.

He rushed down a hallway, knocking out several guards along the way. Suddenly, he came to a stop. Ahead, he saw a man wearing a lab coat rushing out of a room, looking nervous. Once the man was out of sight, Steve walked into the room.

It was full of files, specimen jars, and other medical equipment. In the center of the room was a large cage. And inside that cage was a man.

"Barnes, James Buchanan," the man said, his voice cracking.

Bucky was alive! Racing over, Steve freed his old friend. When Bucky saw the new Steve, his eyes grew wide.

"What happened to you?" he asked.

"I joined the army," Steve answered.

Suddenly, another blast ripped through the building. It was time to go. As they raced for the door, Steve noticed a map on the wall. There were HYDRA symbols all over it, spreading across Europe. He'd have to tell Phillips about that later.

Together, Steve and Bucky made their way down the hall toward the stairs. But another blast caved in the wall, blocking their way. Turning, they headed toward a catwalk, hoping to go above the danger. But they were in for a surprise—Johann Schmidt was standing there, waiting.

The HYDRA leader took a step forward, the light causing his sunken eyes to look even hollower. His face resembled a red skull.

Then, with an evil laugh, Schmidt escaped in an elevator, leaving Bucky and Steve on the catwalk.

More explosions rocked the building as the friends tried to get away. They had almost made it when another bomb blew up the walkway, separating Steve from Bucky. "Just get out!" Steve cried.

Bucky didn't want to go, but he had no choice. He turned to leave as Steve backed up. Then he began to run toward the hole. He was going to jump!

Just as he did, the biggest explosion yet went off. As Bucky watched in horror, Steve disappeared in a fiery inferno. . . .

Back at the US camp, Peggy stood in Phillips's tent, her face drawn. On a typewriter, Phillips had written: "Regret to report Cpt. Steven Rogers, K.I.A. killed in action."

There had been no news of the rescue mission, and everyone believed Captain America had died in action. Suddenly, there was a commotion outside as a group of soldiers ran by. Peggy made her way over to the window. When she looked out, her eyes grew wide.

Steve was walking up to the camp, leading a squad of rescued men—including Bucky. Peggy's heart pounded. He had done it!

As she watched the other soldiers come up and congratulate him, she traded looks with Phillips. He couldn't deny it now. Captain America was an authentic hero.

A few days later, Steve found himself in the SSR's London headquarters. As Peggy, Phillips, and Stark looked on, he sketched the precise coordinates he'd seen on the map in one of the HYDRA labs.

"These are all HYDRA's factories?" Phillips asked Steve.

"Not all of them," Steve answered. "Bucky—Sergeant Barnes—said HYDRA shipped all of their bombs somewhere else. Somewhere not on this map."

Phillips nodded. If HYDRA had more bombs as powerful as the one that destroyed their factory, they had to be stopped. "What do you say, Rogers?" he said. "It's your map. Think you can wipe HYDRA off of it?"

Steve nodded. He wouldn't have it any other way.

Steve quickly put together a team. They were almost ready to go when Stark called Steve down to his lab. He had something to give him.

It was a uniform made of the most high-tech material available. It was flexible, insulated, and fire-resistant.

Steve was impressed. But Stark wasn't done. He walked over to a tarp-covered table and pulled away the fabric. Underneath was a round metallic shield. Steve gingerly reached out to touch it.

"Vibranium," Stark explained. "A hundred times stronger than steel and one third the weight."

As Steve slid it onto his arm, a huge grin spread across his face. He was ready. HYDRA didn't stand a chance.

For the next year, Captain America and his team of Howling Commandos traveled all over Europe, taking down various HYDRA factories. In Czechoslovakia, the team watched as Captain America crashed his motorcycle right through a window, while a factory exploded behind him. They went to France and Greece and Germany, getting better and better.

Finally, Cap and the team made it to Russia. They had gotten intel that a train would be passing by carrying HYDRA's largest shipment of weapons yet—along with their top scientist. Captain America and his men made sure the train never reached its destination.

Instead, they captured several HYDRA foot soldiers, along with some of their most important scientists.

Back at headquarters, Steve listened as Phillips filled them in on the information that the army had received from the captured HYDRA agents. "Johann Schmidt thinks he's a god," the colonel said. "And he's going to blow up half the world to prove it."

Peggy nodded and pointed at a map. "Starting with the United States," she said.

Steve hadn't said anything while the others talked. But he knew what they were thinking. With all its soldiers fighting in the Pacific or Europe, the nation's borders were wide open. He was their only hope.

"Where is Red Skull now?" Steve asked.

Phillips pointed to a photo tacked on the wall. "HYDRA's last base is here, in the Alps." He traced his finger down the map. "Five hundred feet below the surface."

Steve nodded. It wouldn't be easy. But what choice did he have?

A few days later, Captain America raced through the Alps on his motorcycle. He was getting close to the base. He just had to avoid getting captured.

Alarms were sounding as Captain America approached the secret HYDRA factory. Pulling back on the handlebars, he jumped his bike up and over the wall, landing with a crash on the ground inside. Guards fired, and Cap ducked and weaved. But his front tire was hit, and he went flying over the handlebars. Before he knew it, he was surrounded.

He'd been captured.

Captain America soon found himself face-to-face with Red Skull. The HYDRA leader looked pleased. He kicked the Super-Soldier in the face, then smashed him into a concrete wall. Captain America tried to fight back, but Red Skull was too strong.

Schmidt pulled out a gun and aimed. His finger twitched on the trigger when suddenly—BOOM!—there was a loud explosion as the Howling Commandos crashed through the windows. In the chaos, Schmidt raced out of the room.

One of his team members threw Captain America his shield. Using its sharp edges, Cap freed himself and then raced off after Red Skull.

He wasn't going to let the HYDRA leader get away again.

Captain America ran down the hall. Up ahead, Red Skull dashed through a doorway and pushed a button to close the blast doors. Captain America hurled his shield just in time, propping the doors open.

Slipping under them, Cap found himself inside a large hanger. There were five giant planes parked there, each one full of bombs to be dropped on the United States. Suddenly, a huge rumble shook the base as one of the planes rolled past. Schmidt was in the cockpit, a smile on his evil red face.

As Captain America watched, the plane picked up speed. He tried to catch it, but even with all his super strength, he was falling behind. Up ahead, doors opened, letting in the glare of sunlight.

Just then, Captain America heard a rumbling from behind him. Turning around, he saw Colonel Phillips and Peggy driving Red Skull's black car! Without missing a beat, Captain America leaped onto the speeding vehicle. When it was right next to the plane's tire, Captain America took a deep breath. Then he jumped.

Captain America barely managed to grab hold of the landing gear before the plane burst through the open doors and out into the sunshine. A moment later, the gear retracted.

Captain America found himself on the plane's flight deck. And he wasn't alone. There were eight fighter planes in there with him, armed and at the ready—along with eight HYDRA pilots. Seeing Captain America, they rushed forward, blasting their guns.

When they were almost on top of him, Captain America took out two of the pilots. Then he tossed another one across the deck and out of the plane, and knocked out a fourth using his shield. He soon took out the rest and then headed for the cockpit.

It was time to take care of Red Skull.

Captain America knew he had to stop Red Skull from bombing the United States. Then he could come back and take care of the rest of HYDRA.

He would do it for Dr. Erskine, who gave his life to make Steve a Super-Soldier. He would do it for Colonel Phillips, who had finally believed in him. He would do it for Peggy Carter, who had always believed in him.

But most importantly, he would do it for his country and for all the men who had lost their lives.

HE HAD TO. HE WAS CAPTAIN AMERICA.